Zap!

Written by Caroline Harris
Illustrated by Neil Sutherland, Blue-Zoo and Tony Trimmer

Z must go to bed.
He has to nap.

pop!

Z begins to nap, but
I and P pop by.

Will **I** and **P** help?

z-**i**-**p**, zip!

Z can not nap on a zip!
But A has a plan.

z-a-p , zap!

It zaps Z!

Can B and U help Z get
to bed?

b-**u**-**zz**, buzz!

It is a din. It is no help!

J jumps up.

j-**a**-**zz**, jazz!

Will jazz help z get to bed?

Yes! Z gets a rest!

Pixie Ma a Friend

Written by Chitra Soundar

Illustrated by Debasmita Dasgupta

Collins

One day, Pixie picked up a dull,
grey lamp in the field. Pixie rubbed
the lamp. Bea came out of the lamp.

"I'm Bea," she said.

"I'm Pixie," said Pixie. "Can I wish on this lamp?"

"Not until we clean it," said Bea. "Help me make the lamp gleam, Pixie!"

"I'll help you," said Pixie. "We are a team."

6

Pixie and Bea reached the stream.
Pixie dipped in a hankie and rubbed
the lamp.

The lamp still didn't gleam.
"I will polish it," said Pixie.

8

She polished the lamp. It still didn't gleam.

boot
polish

9

"What shall we do now?" asked Pixie.

"We can read some stories," said Bea.

Pixie liked reading stories. Reading was a treat.

Bea reached for a book of stories.
She started to read the tale of seals
that swam in the deep sea.

"Fantastic!" said Pixie.

"It's my turn now!" said Pixie, reaching for the book of stories.

Pixie and Bea took turns to read lots of stories.

The stories were a treat for Pixie and Bea.
They forgot the lamp.

But that night, the lamp started to gleam like starlight.

17

"Now you will get wishes, Pixie!" said Bea.
Pixie leapt with delight.

18

"What wishes will I make?" said Pixie, reaching for the lamp.

"I wish for heaps of books with stories to read!" said Pixie.

"I wish for us to be friends for ever!" said Bea.

What did Pixie do to make the lamp gleam?

23

After reading

Letters and Sounds: Phase 5

Word count: 240

Focus phonemes: /ai/ ay, ey, a-e /ee/ ie, ea

Common exception words: I, liked, the, of, to, are, me, my, we, said, one, do, were, what, friend, be, asked, some, you, out

Curriculum links: PSHE

National Curriculum learning objectives: Reading/word reading: read accurately by blending sounds in unfamiliar words containing GPCs that have been taught; read common exception words, noting unusual correspondences between spelling and sound and where these occur in a word; read words containing taught GPCs; read words with contractions, and understand that the apostrophe represents the omitted letter(s); Reading/comprehension: understand both the books they can already read accurately and fluently and those they listen to by checking that the text makes sense to them as they read, and correcting inaccurate reading

Developing fluency

- Your child may enjoy hearing you read the book.
- Read the narrator's words together but each take a part, one of you reading Pixie's spoken words, the other Bea's.

Phonic practice

- Turn to page 2 and ask your child to find the words that contain the /ee/ sound. Remind them to look out for different ways in which it is written. (*Pixie, field, Bea*)
- Ask your child to read these /ee/ words too. Point out that **she** and **we** are common exception words and do not have an /ee/ spelling that they are used to.

    stream   seals   stories   reaching   hankie   she   we

Extending vocabulary

- Look at pages 3 and 4 and find the word **I'm** on both pages. Ask your child what this is short for. (*I am*)
- Can they work out what letter or letters are missing from these words too?

    it's (*it is*)   he's (*he is*)   she's (*she is*)   that's (*that is*)